Holt Owlet Books is a paperback picture book series, carefully chosen for merit and popularity from a distinguished backlist of children's literature.

Owlet Titles You May Enjoy:

Alexander, Lloyd
    COLL AND HIS WHITE PIG
    THE TRUTHFUL HARP

Belting, Natalia
    THE SUN IS A GOLDEN EARRING

Caudill, Rebecca
    A CERTAIN SMALL SHEPHERD
    DID YOU CARRY THE FLAG
        TODAY, CHARLEY?
    A POCKETFUL OF CRICKET
    THE BEST-LOVED DOLL
    COME ALONG!

Cole, William
    WHAT'S GOOD FOR A FOUR-YEAR-OLD?
    WHAT'S GOOD FOR A FIVE-YEAR-OLD?
    WHAT'S GOOD FOR A SIX-YEAR-OLD?

Jacobs, Leland
    ALPHABET OF GIRLS
    IS SOMEWHERE ALWAYS FAR AWAY?

Johnson, Crockett
    WE WONDER WHAT WILL WALTER BE?
        WHEN HE GROWS UP

Ness, Evaline
    SAM, BANGS AND MOONSHINE
    MR. MIACCA

NicLeodhas, Sorche
    ALWAYS ROOM FOR ONE MORE
    ALL IN THE MORNING EARLY

Stockton, Frank
    THE BEE-MAN OF ORN
    THE GRIFFIN AND THE MINOR CANNON

Wahl, Jan
    CABBAGE MOON
    COBWEB CASTLE

Wondriska, William
    JOHN JOHN TWILLIGER
    MR. BROWN AND MR. GRAY

The Griffin and the Minor Canon

The Griffin and the Minor Canon

BY FRANK R. STOCKTON

WITH ILLUSTRATIONS

BY MAURICE SENDAK

Holt, Rinehart and Winston

New York / Chicago / San Francisco

A Holt Owlet Book

ABOUT THE AUTHOR *by Maurice Sendak*

FRANK R. STOCKTON was born in Philadelphia on April 5, 1834. Although he showed a lively talent for writing at an early age, his parents chose to have him trained, with his brother John, as an engraver. He worked at this craft from 1852 to about 1866, but his real passion remained writing. In 1870, *Ting-a-Ling Tales*, a group of fairy tales, was published by Scribner's; and in 1873, Stockton became assistant editor to Mary Mapes Dodge on *St. Nicholas* magazine, to which, after he gave up editorial work in 1881, he remained a steady contributor.

The first twenty years of *St. Nicholas* reflected a kind of golden age of children's writing. On its pages appeared such names as Howard Pyle, Louisa May Alcott, Sarah Orne Jewett, Joel Chandler Harris, and Frances Hodgson Burnett. Frank Stockton's imaginative tales had an honourable place among these notables, and it is sad that most of his work is unknown to children today. He is remembered for such adult works as "The Lady or the Tiger?" and *Rudder Grange*.

As the artist illustrating Frank Stockton, I had first to discover him as a writer. He had always been, quite honestly, "The Lady or the Tiger?" man. I had never read anything else. Reading "The Griffin and the Minor Canon" was very much like opening a treasure chest. What a gold mine of pictorial possibilities! And it provided a thoroughly fascinating series of illustrating problems. I wanted at all costs to avoid the serious pitfall of illustrating with pictures what the author had already—and so wonderfully—illustrated with words. I hoped, rather, to let the story speak for itself, with my pictures as a kind of background music—music in the right style, in the best taste, and always in tune with the words.

A most bewildering problem had to do with historical (or mythical) fact versus Frank Stockton! Simply: does a griffin have hind legs or does it not? I chose the legs. And being an illustrator who does not arbitrarily deviate from a text, I feel obliged to give my reasons for doing so. My dictionary's definition of griffin, griffon, or gryphon, and all my other research, clearly showed that the griffin, from earliest descriptions, had the rear, tail, and hind paws of a lion. Yet, at the beginning of the story, Mr. Stockton describes the creature as having no hind legs.

Frank Stockton seemingly took the liberty of improvising on the traditional griffin. I took the liberty of improvising on Frank Stockton. Besides the weight of scholarly tradition, there was a purely aesthetic reason for this improvisation. Our friend the griffin is strong, proud, imperious, vain, intelligent, good—and, best of all, lion-hearted. Such a creature loses in dignity when his body dwindles weakly into a serpent's tail.

I think Mr. Stockton would have enjoyed this little commotion over his griffin's anatomy. It so nicely suits his wry humour. Wouldn't he have enjoyed the baffled look on his illustrator's face!

"The Lady or the Tiger?" "The Legs or the Tail?" Pure Stocktonian!

OVER THE GREAT DOOR of an old, old church, which stood in a quiet town of a faraway land, there was carved in stone the figure of a large griffin. The old-time sculptor had done his work with great care, but the image he had made was not a pleasant one to look at. It had a large head, with enormous open mouth and savage teeth; from its back arose great wings,

7

armed with sharp hooks and prongs; it had stout legs in front, with projecting claws; but there were no legs behind—the body running out into a long and powerful tail, finished off at the end with a barbed point. This tail was coiled up under it, the end sticking up just behind its wings.

The sculptor, or the people who had ordered his stone figure, had evidently been very much pleased with it, for little copies of it, also in stone, had been placed here and there along the sides of the church not very far from the ground, so that people could easily look at them and ponder on their curious forms. There were a great many other sculptures on the outside of this church—saints, martyrs, grotesque heads of men, beasts, and birds, as well as those of other creatures which cannot be named, because nobody knows exactly what they were—but none were so curious and interesting as the great griffin over the door and the little griffins on the sides of the church.

A long, long distance from the town, in the midst of

dreadful wilds scarcely known to man, there dwelt the Griffin whose image had been put up over the church door. In some way or other, the old-time sculptor had seen him, and afterward, to the best of his memory, had copied his figure in stone. The Griffin had never known this until, hundreds of years afterward, he heard from a bird, from a wild animal, or in some manner which it is not now easy to find out, that there was a likeness of him on the old church in the distant town.

Now, this Griffin had no idea how he looked. He had never seen a mirror, and the streams where he lived were so turbulent and violent that a quiet piece of water, which would reflect the image of anything looking into it, could not be found. Being, as far as could be ascertained, the very last of his race, he had never seen another griffin. Therefore, it was that when he heard of this stone image of himself, he became very anxious to know what he looked like, and at last determined to go to the old church and see for himself what manner of being he was. So he started

off from the dreadful wilds, and flew on and on until he came to the countries inhabited by men, where his appearance in the air created great consternation; but he alighted nowhere, keeping up a steady flight until he reached the suburbs of the town which had his image on its church. Here, late in the afternoon, he alighted in a green meadow by the side of a brook and stretched himself on the grass to rest. His great wings were tired, for he had not made such a long flight for a century or more.

The news of his coming spread quickly over the town, and the people, frightened nearly out of their wits by the arrival of so extraordinary a visitor, fled into their houses and shut themselves up. The Griffin called loudly for someone to come to him, but the more he called, the more afraid the people were to show themselves. At length, he saw two labourers hurrying to their homes through the fields, and in a terrible voice he commanded them to stop. Not daring to disobey, the men stood, trembling.

"What is the matter with you all?" cried the

Griffin. "Is there not a man in your town who is brave
enough to speak to me?"

"I think," said one of the labourers, his voice shaking
so that his words could hardly be understood, "that—
perhaps—the Minor Canon—would come."

"Go, call him then!" said the Griffin. "I want to
see him."

The Minor Canon, who filled a subordinate position in the old church, had just finished the afternoon services and was coming out of the church with three aged women who had formed the weekday congregation. He was a young man of a kind disposition, and very anxious to do good to the people of the town. Apart from his duties in the church, where he conducted services every weekday, he visited the sick and the poor, counselled and assisted persons who were in trouble, and taught a school composed entirely of the bad children in the town with whom nobody else would have anything to do. Whenever the people wanted something difficult done for them, they always went to the Minor Canon. Thus it was that the labourer thought of the young priest, when he found that someone must come and speak to the Griffin.

The Minor Canon had not heard of the strange event, which was known to the whole town except himself and the three old women, and when he was informed of it and was told that the Griffin had asked to see him, he was greatly amazed and frightened.

"Me!" he exclaimed. "He has never heard of me! What should he want with me?"

"Oh, you must go instantly!" cried the two men. "He is very angry now because he has been kept waiting so long; and nobody knows what may happen if you don't hurry to him."

The poor Minor Canon would rather have had his hand cut off than go out to meet an angry griffin; but he felt that it was his duty to go, for it would be a woeful thing if injury should come to the people of the town because he was not brave enough to obey the summons of the Griffin. So, pale and frightened, he started off.

"Well," said the Griffin, as soon as the young man came nearer, "I am glad to see that there is someone who has the courage to come to me."

The Minor Canon did not feel very courageous, but he bowed his head.

"Is this the town," said the Griffin, "where there is a church with a likeness of myself over one of the doors?"

The Minor Canon looked at the frightful creature before him and saw that he was, without doubt, exactly like the stone image on the church. "Yes," he said, "you are right."

"Well, then," said the Griffin, "will you take me to it? I wish very much to see it."

The Minor Canon instantly thought that if the Griffin entered the town without the people knowing what he came for, some of them would probably be frightened to death, and so he sought to gain time to prepare their minds.

"It is growing dark now," he said, very much afraid, as he spoke, that his words might enrage the Griffin, "and objects on the front of the church cannot be seen clearly.

It will be better to wait until morning, if you wish to get a good view of the stone image of yourself."

"That will suit me very well," said the Griffin. "I see you are a man of good sense. I am tired, and I will take a nap here on this soft grass while I cool my tail in the little stream that runs near me. The end of my tail gets red hot when I am angry or excited, and it is quite warm now. So you may go; but be sure and come early tomorrow morning and show me the way to the church."

The Minor Canon was glad enough to take his leave, and hurried into the town. In front of the church he found a great many people assembled to hear his report of his interview with the Griffin. When they found that the creature had not come to spread ruin and devastation, but simply to see his stony likeness on the church, they showed neither relief nor gratification, but began to up-braid the Minor Canon for consenting to conduct the creature into the town.

"What could I do?" cried the young man. "If I

should not bring him, he would come himself, and perhaps end by setting fire to the town with his red-hot tail.''

Still the people were not satisfied, and a great many plans were proposed to prevent the Griffin from coming into the town. Some elderly persons urged that the young men should go out and kill him; but the young men scoffed at such a ridiculous idea. Then someone said that it would be a good thing to destroy the stone image so that the Griffin would have no excuse for entering the town; and this proposal was received with such favour that many of the people ran for hammers, chisels, and crowbars, with which to tear down and break up the stone griffin. But the Minor Canon resisted this plan with all the strength of his mind and body. He assured the people that this action would enrage the Griffin beyond measure, for it would be impossible to conceal from him that his image had been destroyed during the night. But the people were so determined to break up the stone griffin that the Minor Canon saw that there was nothing for him to do but to stay there and protect it. All night he walked up and down in front of the church door, keeping away the men who brought ladders by which they might mount to the great stone griffin and knock it to pieces with their hammers and crowbars. After many hours, the people were obliged to give up their attempts and went home to sleep; but the Minor Canon remained at his post till early morning, and then he hurried away to the field where he had left the Griffin.

The monster had just awakened, and rising to his forelegs and shaking himself, he said that he was ready to go into the town. The Minor Canon therefore walked back, the Griffin flying slowly through the air at a short distance above the head of his guide. Not a person was to be seen in the streets, and they proceeded directly to the front of the church, where the Minor Canon pointed out the stone griffin.

The real Griffin settled down in the little square before the church and gazed earnestly at his sculptured likeness. For a long time he looked at it. First he put his head on one side, and then he put it on the other; then he shut his right eye and gazed with his left, after which he shut his left eye and gazed with his right. Then he moved a little to one side and looked at the image, then he moved the other way. After a while he said to the Minor Canon, who had been standing by all this time, "It is, it must be, an excellent likeness! That breadth between the eyes, that expansive forehead, those massive jaws! I feel that it must resemble me. If there is any fault to find with it, it is that the neck seems a little stiff. But that is nothing. It is an admirable likeness—admirable!"

The Griffin sat looking at his image all the morning and all the afternoon. The Minor Canon had been afraid to go away and leave him, and had hoped all through the day that he would soon be satisfied with his inspection and fly away home. But by evening, the poor young man

24

was utterly exhausted and felt that he must eat and sleep. He frankly admitted this fact to the Griffin, and asked him if he would not like something to eat. He said this because he felt obliged in politeness to do so, but as soon as he had spoken the words, he was seized with dread lest the monster should demand half-a-dozen babies or some tempting repast of that kind.

25

"Oh, no," said the Griffin. "I never eat between the equinoxes. At the vernal and at the autumnal equinox I take a good meal, and that lasts me for half a year. I am extremely regular in my habits, and do not think it healthful to eat at odd times. But if you need food, go and get it, and I will return to the soft grass where I slept last night and take another nap."

The next day, the Griffin came again to the little square before the church and remained there until evening, steadfastly regarding the stone griffin over the door. The Minor Canon came once or twice to look at him, and the Griffin seemed very glad to see him; but the young clergyman could not stay as he had done before, for he had many duties to perform. Nobody went to the church,

26

but the people came to the Minor Canon's house and anxiously asked him how long the Griffin was going to stay.

"I do not know," he answered, "but I think he will soon be satisfied with regarding his stone likeness and then he will go away."

But the Griffin did not go away. Morning after morning he came to the church, but after a time he did not stay there all day. He seemed to have taken a great fancy to the Minor Canon, and followed him about as he pursued his various avocations. He would wait for him at the side door of the church, for the Minor Canon held services every day, morning and evening, though nobody came now.

"If anyone should come," he said to himself, "I must be found at my post."

When the young man came out, the Griffin would accompany him on his visits to the sick and the poor, and would often look into the windows of the schoolhouse where the Minor Canon was teaching his unruly scholars. All the other schools were closed, but the parents of the Minor Canon's scholars forced them to go to school, because they were so bad they could not endure them all day at home—Griffin or no Griffin. But it must be said they generally behaved very well when that great monster sat up on his tail and looked in at the schoolroom window.

When it was perceived that the Griffin showed no signs of going away, all the people who were able to do so left the town. The canons and the higher officers of the church had fled away during the first day of the Griffin's visit, leaving behind only the Minor Canon and some of the men who opened the doors and swept the church. All the citizens who could afford it shut up their houses and travelled to distant parts, and only the working people and the poor were left behind. After some days, these ventured to go about and attend to their business, for if they did not work, they would starve. They were getting a little used to seeing the Griffin, and having been told that he did not eat between equinoxes, they did not feel so much afraid of him as before.

Day by day, the Griffin became more and more attached to the Minor Canon. He kept near him a great part of the time, and often spent the night in front of the little house where the young clergyman lived alone. This strange companionship was often burdensome to the

29

Minor Canon; but, on the other hand, he could not deny that he derived a great deal of benefit and instruction from it. The Griffin had lived for hundreds of years, and had seen much, and he told the Minor Canon many wonderful things.

"It is like reading an old book," said the young clergyman to himself; "but how many books I would have had to read before I would have found out what the Griffin has told me about the earth, the air, the water, about minerals, and metals, and growing things, and all the wonders of the world!"

30

Thus the summer went on, and drew toward its close. And now the people of the town began to be very much troubled again.

"It will not be long," they said, "before the autumnal equinox is here, and then that monster will want to eat. He will be dreadfully hungry, for he has taken so much exercise since his last meal. He will devour our children. Without doubt, he will eat them all. What is to be done?"

To this question no one could give an answer, but all agreed that the Griffin must not be allowed to remain until the approaching equinox. After talking over the matter a great deal, a crowd of the people went to the Minor Canon at a time when the Griffin was not with him.

"It is all your fault," they said, "that that monster is among us. You brought him here, and you ought to see that he goes away. It is only on your account that he stays here at all, for, although he visits his image every day, he is with you the greater part of the time. If you were not here, he would not stay. It is your duty to go

away and then he will follow you, and we shall be free from the dreadful danger which hangs over us."

"Go away!" cried the Minor Canon, greatly grieved at being spoken to in such a way. "Where shall I go? If I go to some other town, shall I not take this trouble there? Have I a right to do that?"

"No," said the people, "you must not go to any other town. There is no town far enough away. You must go to the dreadful wilds where the Griffin lives; and then he will follow you and stay there."

They did not say whether or not they expected the Minor Canon to stay there also, and he did not ask them anything about it. He bowed his head, and went into his house to think. The more he thought, the more clear it became to his mind that it was his duty to go away and thus free the town from the presence of the Griffin.

That evening, he packed a leathern bag full of bread and meat, and early the next morning he set out on his journey to the dreadful wilds. It was a long, weary, and

32

doleful journey, especially after he had gone beyond the habitations of men, but the Minor Canon kept on bravely and never faltered. The way was longer than he had expected, and his provisions soon grew so scanty that he was obliged to eat but a little every day, but he kept up his courage and pressed on, and, after many days of toilsome travel, he reached the dreadful wilds.

When the Griffin found that the Minor Canon had left the town, he seemed sorry, but showed no disposition to go and look for him. After a few days had passed, he became much annoyed, and asked some of the people where the Minor Canon had gone. But, although the citizens had been so anxious that the young clergyman should go to the dreadful wilds, thinking that the Griffin would immediately follow him, they were now afraid to mention the Minor Canon's destination, for the monster seemed angry already, and, if he should suspect their trick, he would doubtless become very much enraged. So every one said he did not know, and the Griffin wandered about disconsolate. One morning he looked into the Minor Canon's schoolhouse, which was always empty now, and thought that it was a shame that everything should suffer on account of the young man's absence.

"It does not matter so much about the church," he said, "for nobody went there; but it is a pity about the school. I think I will teach it myself until he returns."

It was the hour for opening the school, and the Griffin went inside and pulled the rope which rang the school bell. Some of the children who heard the bell ran in to see what was the matter, supposing it to be a joke of one of their companions; but when they saw the Griffin they stood astonished and scared.

"Go tell the other scholars," said the monster, "that school is about to open, and that if they are not all here in ten minutes I shall come after them."

In seven minutes, every scholar was in place.

Never was seen such an orderly school. Not a boy or girl moved or uttered a whisper. The Griffin climbed

into the master's seat, his wide wings spread on each side of him, because he could not lean back in his chair while they stuck out behind, and his great tail coiled around in front of the desk, the barbed end sticking up ready to tap any boy or girl who might misbehave.

The Griffin now addressed the scholars, telling them that he intended to teach them while their master was away. In speaking, he tried to imitate, as far as possible, the mild and gentle tones of the Minor Canon; but it must be admitted that in this he was not very successful.

He had paid a good deal of attention to the studies of the school, and he determined not to try to teach them anything new, but to review them in what they had been studying; so he called up the various classes and questioned them upon their previous lessons. The children racked their brains to remember what they had learned. They were so afraid of the Griffin's displeasure that they recited as they had never recited before. One of the boys, far down in his class, answered so well that the Griffin was astonished.

"I should think you would be at the head," said he. "I am sure you have never been in the habit of reciting so well. Why is this?"

"Because I did not choose to take the trouble," said the boy, trembling in his boots. He felt obliged to speak the truth, for all the children thought that the great eyes of the Griffin could see right through them, and that he would know when they told a falsehood.

"You ought to be ashamed of yourself," said the

Griffin. "Go down to the very tail of the class; and if you are not at the head in two days, I shall know the reason why."

The next afternoon this boy was Number One.

It was astonishing how much these children now learned of what they had been studying. It was as if they had been educated over again. The Griffin used no severity toward them, but there was a look about him which made them unwilling to go to bed until they were sure they knew their lessons for the next day.

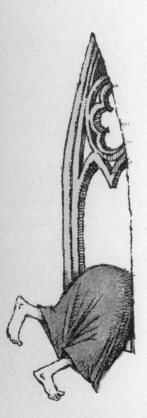

The Griffin now thought that he ought to visit the sick and the poor; and he began to go about the town for this purpose. The effect upon the sick was miraculous. All, except those who were very ill indeed, jumped from their beds when they heard he was coming, and declared themselves quite well. To those who could not get up, he gave herbs and roots, which none of them had ever before thought of as medicines, but which the Griffin had seen used in various parts of the world; and most of them

recovered. But, for all that, they afterward said that no matter what happened to them, they hoped that they should never again have such a doctor coming to their bedsides, feeling their pulses and looking at their tongues.

As for the poor, they seemed to have utterly disappeared. All those who had depended upon charity for their daily bread were now at work in some way or other, many of them offering to do odd jobs for their neighbours, just for the sake of their meals—a thing which before had been seldom heard of in the town. The Griffin could find no one who needed his assistance.

The summer had now passed, and the autumnal equinox was rapidly approaching. The citizens were in a

40

state of great alarm and anxiety. The **Griffin** showed **no** signs of going away, but seemed to have settled himself permanently among them. In a short time the day for his semiannual meal would arrive, and then what would happen? The monster would certainly be very hungry, and would devour all their children.

Now, they greatly regretted and lamented that they had sent away the Minor Canon; he was the only one on whom they could have depended in this trouble, for he could talk freely with the Griffin and so find out what could be done. But it would not do to be inactive. Some step must be taken immediately. A meeting of the citizens was called, and two old men were appointed to go and

41

talk to the Griffin. They were instructed to offer to prepare a splendid dinner for him on equinox day—one which would entirely satisfy his hunger. They would offer him the fattest mutton, the most tender beef, fish and game of various sorts, and anything of the kind that he might fancy. If none of these suited, they were to mention that there was an orphan asylum in the next town.

"Anything would be better," said the citizens, "than to have our dear children devoured."

The old men went to the Griffin; but their propositions were not received with favour.

"From what I have seen of the people of this town," said the monster, "I do not think I could relish anything which was prepared by them. They appear to be all cowards, and, therefore, mean and selfish. As for eating one of them, old or young, I could not think of it for a moment. In fact, there was only one creature in the whole place for whom I could have had any appetite, and that was the Minor Canon, who has gone away. He was brave and

42

good and honest, and I think I should have relished him.''

"Ah!" said one of the old men very politely, "in that case I wish we had not sent him to the dreadful wilds!"

"What!" cried the Griffin. "What do you mean? Explain instantly what you are talking about!"

The old man, terribly frightened at what he had said, was obliged to tell how the Minor Canon had been sent away by the people, in the hope that the Griffin might be induced to follow him.

When the monster heard this, he became furiously angry. He dashed away from the old men, and, spreading his wings, flew backward and forward over the town. He

43

was so much excited that his tail became red hot and glowed like a meteor against the evening sky. When at last he settled down in the little field where he usually rested and thrust his tail into the brook, the steam arose like a cloud and the water of the stream ran hot through the town. The citizens were greatly frightened, and bitterly blamed the old man for telling the Griffin about the Minor Canon.

"It is plain," they said, "that the Griffin intended at last to go and look for him, and we should have been saved. Now, who can tell what misery you have brought upon us?"

The Griffin did not remain long in the little field. As soon as his tail was cool, he flew to the town hall and rang the bell. The citizens knew that they were expected to come there; and although they were afraid to go, they were still more afraid to stay away, and they crowded

46

into the hall. The Griffin was on the platform at one end, flapping his wings and walking up and down, and the end of his tail was still so warm that it slightly scorched the boards as he dragged it after him.

When everybody who was able to come was there, the Griffin stood still and addressed the meeting.

"I have had a very low opinion of you," he said, "ever since I discovered what cowards you are, but I had no idea that you were so ungrateful, selfish, and cruel as I now find you to be. Here was your Minor Canon, who

laboured day and night for your good, and thought of nothing else but how he might benefit you and make you happy; and as soon as you imagine yourselves threatened with a danger—for well I know you are dreadfully afraid of me—you send him off, caring not whether he returns or perishes, hoping thereby to save yourselves. Now, I had conceived a great liking for that young man, and had intended, in a day or two, to go and look him up. But I have changed my mind about him. I shall go and find him, but I shall send him back here to live among you, and I intend that he shall enjoy the reward of his labour and his sacrifices.

"Go, some of you, to the officers of the church, who were so cowardly as to run away when I first came here, and tell them never to return to this town under penalty of death. And if, when your Minor Canon comes back to you, you do not bow yourselves before him, put him in the highest place among you, and serve and honour him all his life, beware of my terrible vengeance! There were only two good things in this town: the Minor Canon and the stone image of myself over your church door. One of these you have sent away, and the other I shall carry away myself."

With these words he dismissed the meeting; and it

was time, for the end of his tail had become so hot that there was danger of its setting fire to the building.

The next morning the Griffin came to the church, and tearing the stone image of himself from its fastenings over the great door, he grasped it with his powerful fore-legs and flew up into the air. Then, after hovering over the town for a moment, he gave his tail an angry shake and took up his flight to the dreadful wilds. When he reached this desolate region, he set the stone griffin upon a ledge of a rock which rose in front of the dismal cave he called his home. There, the image occupied a position somewhat similar to that it had had over the church door; and the Griffin, panting with the exertion of carrying such an enormous load so great a distance, lay down upon the ground and regarded it with much satisfaction. When

49

he felt somewhat rested, he went to look for the Minor Canon. He found the young man, weak and half-starved, lying under the shadow of a rock. After picking him up and carrying him to his cave, the Griffin flew away to a distant marsh, where he procured some roots and herbs which he well knew were strengthening and beneficial to man, though he had never tasted them himself. After eating these, the Minor Canon was greatly revived, and sat up and listened while the Griffin told him what had happened in the town.

"Do you know," said the monster, when he had finished, "that I have had, and still have, a great liking for you?"

"I am very glad to hear it," said the Minor Canon, with his usual politeness.

"I am not at all sure that you would be," said the Griffin, "if you thoroughly understood the state of the case; but we will not consider that now. If some things were different, other things would be otherwise. I have been so enraged by discovering the manner in which you have been treated, that I have determined that you shall at last enjoy the rewards and honours to which you are entitled. Lie down and have a good sleep, and then I will take you back to the town."

51

As he heard these words, a look of trouble came over the young man's face.

"You need not give yourself any anxiety," said the Griffin, "about my return to the town. I shall not remain there. Now that I have that admirable likeness of myself in front of my cave, where I can sit at my leisure and gaze upon its noble features, I have no wish to see that abode of cowardly and selfish people."

The Minor Canon, relieved from his fears, lay back, and dropped into a doze; and when he was sound asleep, the Griffin took him up and carried him back to the town. He arrived just before daybreak, and, putting the young man gently on the grass in the little field where he himself used to rest, the monster, without having been seen by any of the people, flew back to his home.

When the Minor Canon made his appearance in the morning among the citizens, the enthusiasm and cordiality with which he was received were truly wonderful.

He was taken to a house which had been occupied by

one of the banished high officers of the place, and every-
one was anxious to do all that could be done for his health
and comfort. The people crowded into the church when
he held services, so that the three old women who used
to be his weekday congregation could not get to the best
seats, which they had always been in the habit of taking;
and the parents of the bad children determined to reform
them at home, in order that he might be spared the
trouble of keeping up his former school. The Minor Canon
was appointed to the highest office of the old church,
and before he died, he became a bishop.

During the first years after his return from the dreadful wilds, the people of the town looked up to him as a
man to whom they were bound to do honour and reverence;
but they often, also, looked up to the sky to see if there
were any signs of the Griffin coming back. However, in
the course of time, they learned to honour and reverence
their former Minor Canon without the fear of being
punished if they did not do so.

But they need never have been afraid of the Griffin. The autumnal equinox came round, and the monster ate nothing. If he could not have the Minor Canon, he did not care for anything. So, lying down, with his eyes fixed upon the great stone griffin, he gradually declined and died. It was a good thing for some of the people of the town that they did not know this.

If you should ever visit the old town, you would still see the little griffins on the sides of the church; but the great stone griffin that was over the door is gone.